My Dad, the Hero

S T E L L A   G U R N E Y

I L L U S T R A T E D   B Y

K A T H A R I N E   M^cE W E N

WALKER
BOOKS

For my lovely little niece, Amelia Rose,
and for my bump, with love
S.G.

For Angus, with love
K.M.

*With special thanks to Imran Khan for his help
and advice on this project*

First published 2008 by Walker Books Ltd
87 Vauxhall Walk, London SE11 5HJ

4 6 8 10 9 7 5

Text © 2008 Stella Gurney
Illustrations © 2008 Katharine McEwen

The right of Stella Gurney and Katharine McEwen to be identified as author
and illustrator respectively of this work has been asserted by them in
accordance with the Copyright, Designs and Patents Act 1988

This book has been typeset in Bembo Educational
and CowsPlain

Printed and bound in China

British Library Cataloguing in Publication Data:
a catalogue record for this book is available from the British Library

ISBN: 978-1-4063-0698-9

www.walker.co.uk

The Very Important Man

GRAND
HOTEL

5

Every day, when Tariq (or "T", as he is known) gets home from school, he runs upstairs to wake his dad.

First he carefully twists the door handle… Then he tiptoes into the dark, shadowy room … quietly … *shh* … over to the big shape snoring beneath the blankets, and …

JUMP!

"Mor-ning!" T yells (even though it's nearly evening).

Dad sits bolt upright with a funny look of surprise. Then he laughs and tickles T and gives him a great big welcome-home bear hug. It's T's favourite part of the day.

On Monday, after T woke him up, Dad had a shower and then began to cook dinner. T had some maths homework to do. He was good at maths; he liked the way the answers to sums slid into his head.

As T worked, he could hear his little sister, Shazia, talking to the dolls Dad had made her.

Dad made all sorts of things in his workshop. Actually it wasn't really a workshop; it was the spare bedroom. When people came to stay, they sometimes found wood shavings in the bed! Dad could carve almost anything.

For T's last birthday
Dad had made him
a beautiful cricket
bat with towelling
tape wrapped
around the handle.
Everyone at school
always wanted
a go on it.

Dad was teaching T how to carve,
but it was a lot harder than
it looked. So far, T had
made an aeroplane
and a boat – although
Mum hadn't been
sure which was which.

13

As he cooked, Dad sang along with a song on the radio. Then Mum came home from work and one of the aunties popped round for a chat. Soon the kitchen was full of talk and steam and delicious smells. T felt very happy.

While they were eating, Dad told
a funny story about a bossy man who
had got into his taxi
last night.

"He was wearing a smart suit with a bow tie, and he said he was on his way to a Very Important Party at the Grand Hotel. I said I knew how to get there, but he wanted to go his way, so eventually I just followed his directions."

Dad began to laugh. T laughed too, even though he didn't know the ending yet.

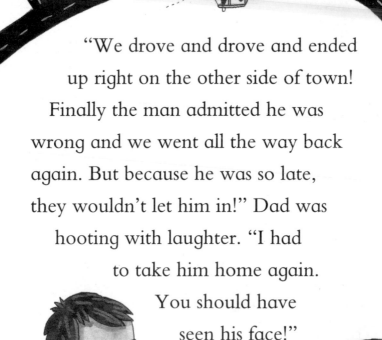

"We drove and drove and ended
up right on the other side of town!
Finally the man admitted he was
wrong and we went all the way back
again. But because he was so late,
they wouldn't let him in!" Dad was
hooting with laughter. "I had
to take him home again.
You should have
seen his face!"

They all fell about on their chairs
laughing at Dad's impression of the
man, even though T didn't like to hear
about ANYONE being rude
to his dad.

Next Mum told them about her day at work. It was her friend Marie's birthday. T's mum had made her some sweets, and someone else had baked a cake. "We wanted to surprise Marie with them in her lunch break," said Mum. "We were

lighting the candles on the
cake, but we were whispering
and giggling so much that
Marie came over and caught us!
She was dead chuffed, though.
And everyone said my
sweets were delicious."

Then it was T's turn. He told them how many runs he'd got playing cricket at lunchtime, and that Tom Morley had said Sophie Mitchell smelled and made everyone laugh at her. Mum said Tom sounded like an idiot.

Finally Shazia told a story, but it wasn't very good because she was only three.

That night, Dad came and kissed
T and Shazia goodnight before he left
for work. T snuggled down under the
covers and sighed happily. When he
was grown up, he wanted to drive
a taxi like his dad. They would beep
at each other when they passed, and
meet for cups of tea to tell stories
about the people they had picked up.

T couldn't wait.

The Big Lie

The next morning, T and Shazia
jumped out of Dad's taxi at the
school gates. Dad had just finished
his night shift and was heading back
home to sleep.

"Bye!" yelled T over his shoulder as he raced into the playground. He could see his friends Jack and Ravinder practising their overarm bowling near the wheelie bins. Shazia's friends were over by the railings.

"Have fun!" called Dad,
waving as he pulled away.
"See you
tonight!"

"'See you tonight! See you tonight!'"
came a voice near by. T turned to see
Tom Morley with two older boys from
another class.

"Why does your dad talk like that?"
Tom grinned. "He sounds stupid."

T couldn't think of anything to say. At home Dad spoke his own language with them – Bengali. When he spoke English he had a strong accent.

T turned and walked away. Tears came to his eyes, but there was no way he was going to let Tom see him cry.

All morning T was very quiet.
He was angry with Tom, but he was
even angrier with himself. Why hadn't
he stood up for his dad? T couldn't
even concentrate in maths, and
Mrs Summers noticed.

"Everything all right, Tariq?"
she asked as she passed his desk.
He nodded, eyes down.

"Well, I've got something that will
cheer you up this afternoon." She
smiled.

T looked up. "What, Miss?"

"Wait and see."

At lunchtime T and his friends played
cricket on the grass. By the time the
whistle went, T was feeling better.
Mum was right – Tom Morley *was* an
idiot. Who cared what he thought?

35

Just before home time,
Mrs Summers called
for quiet.

"I wrote to all your parents a few weeks ago to ask them if they would like to come to speak at our new Friday lessons," she said. "Each week we want to learn about a different kind of job that people do. Lots of your parents replied, and this morning I put all their names in a hat and drew out … Mr Chaudury, Tariq's dad!"

"Tariq's dad is a taxi driver," Mrs Summers continued, "and I'm sure he has lots of interesting things to tell us. Tariq, here is a letter for your father to let him know he's our first guest next Friday."

She handed T an envelope. He sat
holding it as chairs scraped all around
him for home time.

As T laid the table that evening,
the letter still lay in his school bag.
If he gave it to Dad, Dad would want
to do the talk. And if Dad did the talk,
people might laugh at his accent.
T couldn't bear to think of his dad
being mimicked by someone
like Tom. Perhaps he could tell
Mrs Summers that Dad was
too busy to come in…

He took the letter
out of his bag and
put it in the dustbin.

Later, T lay in bed, unable to sleep.
In the kitchen Mum was tidying up.
She saw a letter poking out of the
rubbish. She opened it and took it
to show Dad in his workshop. They
talked for a while. Dad smiled. By the
time T had finally
fallen asleep,
Mum and Dad
had a plan.

The Puppet Show

Bangs and whistles came from Dad's workshop. T stared moodily at the TV. Shazia was watching some stupid baby programme on CBeebies.
T switched over.
Shazia started to howl and Mum came in.

45

"What's going on? Tariq, what have you done to your sister? I don't know what's wrong with you at the moment – you're so grumpy."

T looked at the floor. It was true.
Ever since he had thrown away that
letter he had been miserable, and he
was taking it out on everyone else.

"I'm going up
to my room,"
he mumbled.

He hadn't yet found the courage
to tell Mrs Summers that Dad couldn't
do the talk. He'd decided that when
Dad didn't turn up, he would act as
surprised as everyone else.

But Jack and Ravinder kept asking
which stories T's dad was going to tell.
T was always telling them about Dad's
taxi passengers, and when they came
round they loved listening to his stories.
They thought he was brilliant.
T wanted to tell his friends why he
hadn't given his dad the letter, but
he didn't think they'd understand.

Finally, Friday came. Dad dropped
them off at school as usual. He winked
at T as he got out of the taxi.

"See you later!" He smiled.

Lessons passed slowly. Lunchtime came and went. T prepared himself for his Big Lie. The moment came and his heart thudded.

"Now, class," said Mrs Summers.

"Pens down, please, and quiet. We all need to go to the hall for the first of our special new lessons. Line up by the door, please. QUIETLY!"

T's stomach stopped. There had to be some mistake. He put up his hand but everyone was already moving towards the door. Mrs Summers didn't see him. This was like a bad dream. Slowly T joined the line. The class filed into the hall and sat on the floor in front of the stage.

Standing alone in the middle of the stage was a beautiful wooden puppet theatre. T didn't understand.

The class settled down and waited. Suddenly a miniature taxicab popped up at the front of the theatre, followed by a puppet man in a smart suit.

The puppet began
waving his arms at
the taxi. The taxi stopped,
and the puppet man started talking
loudly, though he wasn't *really* talking,
just making bossy sounds. Every so
often he said, "Grand Hotel!"

The taxi driver made sounds
in reply and T recognized the story:
it was about the night Dad picked up
the rude man on his way to his Very
Important Party. T looked sideways.
All eyes were on the puppets. T looked
back at the stage. By now, the man
was trying to get into the hotel but the
doors were locked. Everyone laughed.

Dad must have been making this in his workshop all week! T's heart filled with love. He felt so proud of Dad and ashamed of himself at the same time. Dad was brilliant. Dad was his hero!

More stories followed, each funnier
than the one before. At last the puppet
show came to an end, and T's class
cheered and clapped. Dad came out
bowing, and Mrs Summers asked if
anyone had any questions.

Everybody put up their hands.
"Tom," chose Mrs Summers.
T held his breath.
"What's the town
like in the middle
of the night?" asked
Tom Morley.

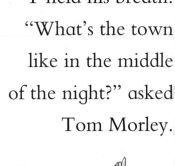

Dad winked at T and
beckoned to him.
T stood up shyly and
squeezed his way to the front.

Dad described what it was like
to drive through the empty streets at
night. He spoke in Bengali. Every few
sentences, he paused and smiled at T,
and T repeated what he said, but in
English. It felt great.

The whole class had questions,
but Mrs Summers said there was just
time for one more surprise. Then T's
mum came out from behind the stage
with two big trays of sweets. Everybody
ran to try one.

Sophie Mitchell asked Dad
if he would do the puppet show
at her birthday party. Ravinder and
Jack asked if he would make them
cricket bats and teach them how to
say "Howzat!" in Bengali.

T held Dad's hand and felt perfectly happy. He tugged on his sleeve. His dad looked down, and T whispered, "I love you, Dad!"

"I know, son," said Dad. "I know." And he squeezed T's hand.